THE BALL, THE BOOK, AND THE DRUM

Story by Morgan Troll

Illustrations by Lori Anderson

To Spike,

Morgan Troll

Raintree Publishers

Milwaukee

In memory of Grandma Korns—she would have been proud;
to my favorite Trolls—David, Linda, Sal, and Ed; and to Janet Lee Hay.   **—M.T**

To my best friends—Brooke, Paul, and Theron.   **—L.A.**

Library of Congress Cataloging-in-Publication Data

Troll, Morgan.
   The ball, the book, and the drum/story by Morgan Troll; illustrations by Lori Anderson.

   Summary: An ugly troll gives up his trollish ways and finds true happiness after he befriends a group of children.
   [1. Trolls—Fiction.]   I. Anderson, Lori, ill.   II. Title.
PZ7.T4845Bal   1990   [Fic]—dc20   90-42443
ISBN 0-8172-2781-4   CIP
                                                      AC

Once upon a time, there lived a troll named Warty Morganson. He was a typical troll—mean, distrustful, and unbelievably ugly. He had a long, black tail and a large, cucumber-shaped nose. He was very strong and fast, and he smelled awful.

Warty, like other trolls, liked to keep boxes and boxes of things that he had stolen. This seemed to make him happy.

Among his stolen treasures were a golden ball, a leather-bound book, and a silver drum with hand-carved drumsticks. These were his prized possessions. Although Warty enjoyed owning these things, he saw no real use for them.

Warty spent many of his days trudging through the woods and fields, looking for new treasures. Sometimes he would even sneak into the nearby village looking for things to collect. On this particular day, he came home empty-handed.

After such bad luck, Warty decided to spend the evening looking at his old treasures. He would try again tomorrow to ruin someone's day by stealing. He hoped that whatever he stole would be greatly missed and would cause the former owners to cry miserably.

With that thought, Warty smiled as he scampered up the dark stairs to his closet filled with stolen treasures.

When Warty reached the top of the stairs, he saw that the closet door was hanging open. Someone had broken in and taken his treasures! Only a woolen glove, a doll, and a broken hoe were left. His favorites were gone! Warty sat down and burst into tears.

"How dare someone steal MY stuff! MY favorites! MINE, MINE, MINE!" Warty shouted.

He spent the night tossing and turning. He could not sleep. Tomorrow he would find the rotten culprit.

Warty was up bright and early the next
morning. He would find the thief and make him pay!

He searched for hours and hours with no luck at
all. The hours turned into days. Warty searched
everywhere. He found many treasures, none of
which were his favorite stolen ones—the ball, the
book, and the drum.

One day, weeks after his loss, Warty heard a strange noise from behind a nearby wall. Then, much to his surprise, Warty saw his golden ball appear up in the air and go back down again. At last! Now he would get the culprit!

Warty quietly crept up a large, leafy tree that hung over the wall. Hidden among the leaves, he could see what was happening on the ground below without being discovered.

Warty saw a human girl child. He did not recognize the strange sounds the child was making as she played. She was running back and forth, tossing the ball into the air. Warty did not know that you could toss anything but gnomes. He liked to do that when he stumbled across the innocent little creatures in the woods. That was great fun for Warty.

Warty looked across the garden. He saw a group of human children. The children were gathered around an older human who was holding Warty's leather-bound book.

What was the older human doing? She was looking at the book and then talking. Warty remembered pictures in the book and thought she must be talking about those pictures.

When the woman stopped to look up, one of the small humans said, "Read some more, Momma. Read some more."

In a far corner of the garden was another human child, who had Warty's silver drum. The child seemed to be enjoying himself, making interesting *tap, tap, tappity, tap, tap* sounds on the drum.

All of the children were having a wonderful time. Much to Warty's surprise, they were not just looking at Warty's things. They were using them. Warty had not realized that the purpose of having things was to enjoy them.

Warty climbed down into the garden. The child nearest him, the one with the ball, dropped it and ran toward some of the other children.

Silence filled the garden, as everyone waited to see what the very ugly troll would do. Warty picked up the ball and tossed it to the little girl. The child realized that Warty was not trying to be mean. She tossed the ball back to him. They began playing catch.

Warty laughed and laughed, just like the little girl. He liked how he felt when he laughed. He had never laughed before.

27

Soon Warty became friends with the children. They explained that they had found his stolen things lying in the garden one day. Warty often could be found playing ball or marching to the beat of the drum with the children. He even learned how to read. He soon gave up his trollish ways. He didn't steal from anyone anymore.

Warty had learned that the best things in life are meant to be shared and enjoyed by all. He discovered that the sounds of laughter and joy that come from sharing are the very best sounds in the world.

Morgan Troll, the author of **The Ball, the Book, and the Drum**, is a student at Maple Ridge Elementary School in Somerset, Pennsylvania. He wrote the story when he was in the fourth grade. Morgan Troll used his name, his imagination, and his own personal philosophies when writing his award-winning story.

The main character of the story, Warty Morganson, is a troll who shares Morgan's interest in sports, reading, and playing drums. Morgan also enjoys playing basketball, soccer, and computer games. As a Cub Scout, he has reached the Arrow of Light rank.

At Maple Ridge, Morgan is a member of the SAGE (Somerset Area Gifted Education) program.

Janet Lee Hay, who sponsored Morgan in Raintree's Publish-A-Book Contest, has been his SAGE teacher. She has been instrumental in motivating Morgan and his classmates to achieve.

Morgan's mother, Linda, is an elementary-school librarian. His father, David, owns a printing business.

Morgan and his parents enjoyed May 4, 1990, when their hometown and the school celebrated "Morgan Troll Day." On that day, students, school administrators and faculty, parents, grandparents, and friends were part of a school program that included Morgan's receiving citations from the mayor, the local state senator, the state House of Representatives, and the lieutenant governor.

Although Morgan has a flair for writing, his career goal is to be a research physician. He would like to discover a cure for cancer.

The twenty honorable-mention winners in the **1990 Raintree Publish-A-Book Contest** were: Della Armstrong of Moyie Springs, Idaho; Alane Benson of McKeesport, Pennsylvania; Jonathan Caton of Flossmoor, Illinois; Gabriel Chrisman of Bainbridge Island, Washington; Christy Druml of Waukesha, Wisconsin; Rebecca L. Emmel of Sandpoint, Idaho; Nicole Estvanik of Enfield, Connecticut; Amanda M. Frank of Slinger, Wisconsin; Lara Garraghty of Goode, Virginia; Andrea Jauregui of Syosset, New York; Aynsley Kenner of Mesa, Arizona; Dharma C. Lawrence of Spring, Texas; Jackie Lyn Leavitt of Idaho Falls, Idaho; Darren Ruthenbeck of Carmichael, California; Tim Schlosser of Durand, Wisconsin; Blake Smisson of Fort Valley, Georgia; Tori Smith of Walkerton, Indiana; Pia Suparak of San Dimas, California; Christy Williams of Mt. Dora, Florida; and Stephanie York of Edmonton, Kentucky.

Artist Lori Anderson was born in California but has spent most of her life in Utah. She lives in Provo, Utah, with her three children—Brooke, Paul, and Theron. Lori has been a professional illustrator for the past twelve years. She also teaches illustration and design at Brigham Young University. In addition to enjoying her family and friends, Lori likes film, drama, hiking, and reading.